Portraits of Time

Andrei Guruianu

Cover art and Illustrations by Teknari

Fomite

Burlington, VT

ISBN-13: 978-1-947917-94-1
Library of Congress Control Number: 2021940948
Fomite
58 Peru Street
Burlington, VT 05401

ACKNOWLEDGMENTS

I extend my gratitude to the readers and editors of the following print and online publications where passages from this collection have appeared previously:

The Prose Poem Project, Yellow Medicine Review, Hawai'i Review, Ginosko, Redactions: Poetry & Poetics, Red Wheel Barrow Poets, Cahoodaloodaling: A Collaborative Publication, Shadowbox, Askew, OCHO, Poets and Artists.

TABLE OF CONTENTS

PART ONE
A Short Biography of Raindrops

Bucharest in June with a bucket when everything disappears through the false bottom. If I had to choose, this one is my favorite story from the library of nightmares. But they are all that good: *Time as the devil of love*; *A madman who divides long enough until there are no remainders*; *The heartbroken widow walking home alone with a gold chain around her neck and an empty locket because she says she is trying to forget.* All of them happening in the gaps between dreams, between seasons, between how it was and how it might have been.

*

Bucharest in June when the eastern skies pour down as if someone threw open the deadbolt of night. As if the sky had never been made of anything else but interminable rain and the near-absence of light. I keep coming back to this one because it resembles most of all the fragile infrastructure of longing. Like a carnival ride that always ends exactly where it begins, a familiar pattern of doubt one no longer questions. By the time the music stops it's gotten so late that it's early, and we turn ugly or beautiful and tender according to each other's needs.

*

Bucharest in June with a bucket when I try to hold the water in my hands by making smaller buckets of skin. But the rain comes down hard, it falls through the false bottom, through the husk of myself like a second skin I've outgrown and which no longer fools anyone. I watch the water pool around my ankles and think to myself, *I can't even remember what it's like not to drown.*

The television mouths in silence something about Spain, something about farthest Russia, about God-knows-where. On most days I would care, but not now. I come here, years later, because they say the coffee is good, and the people know how to dress to complement the architecture.

But it's the same thing every time—couples pair up then walk out holding hands and I think how stupid it is that they can't be compared to anything else but flowers or birds. They are flowers and birds.

The coffee is not that good. Still I drink my cup alone, smoke my cigarettes alone. Some days there are no words. On each table there are empty cups and glasses with their lipstick mouths and their sweet tobacco breath and all their stories punctuated by small rituals and habit.

A sadness beyond belief. Like a long, unending winter loneliness when all of the windows fog over and the ice is as thick as a palm upon the ledge. The night's cold petals wilt and disappear by morning. More flowers that come and go. Thank God that it's a hellish June. At least there are flowers everywhere, on summer dresses, on low-necked blouses, the wallpaper draped in blue ivy.

From the stereo above. one love song blends into another, the notes wistful, predictably tragic: Some of us are forced to die more than once because we have no other choice.

A couple next to me is making plans because they know that now is not enough—her right hand in his left like a rope knotted in the middle and both of them holding on with all of the force they could muster. I leave them like that, the boy who doesn't know what he has in his palm and her painted nails just like that, her mouth just like that, and her hair and her sandals and her…

The heat is done for today, *finis*, it is bearable again. I walk out and wait by the curb, watch every bus come to the station but the one I need. What do I need? Where do I have to go now that I'm here?

Inside the apartment I turn off the light and play a slow and mournful record down to the last groove—in this chair, glass in hand, each song coming to an end as if it were the last and only butterfly in bloom.

When enough distance and enough time has passed all countries reach and call out through the space between, a whisper beautiful and delicate heard in your native tongue. You perch upon the branches of imagination and in a sweeping glance take in the sprawling parks with their lakes and gardens, the avenues and boulevards meandering through all of your melancholy days. And somewhere, down below, there is a girl among the busy streets who'll say, without a hint of the absurd, she read Marquez in Spanish once and knows about true love.

You told me this under a mystic sky of fog and dust, on a rooftop in the middle of a city turning the soft edge of midnight. What did I care about country and time, about books and language and whether love or nostalgia can ever approximate their intimacy? All I knew is that it felt good to brush my arm against yours, eyeing the suggestion of bones, the tragedy of that low plunging line. Your voice landing in the space between us like a new obsession, one I knew could very well be killing me.

Afterward we climbed down and walked the streets for hours and years and millennia, everywhere trailed by ghosts, their chatter indiscernible as so much wind careening through the eaves. None of it made any sense except the gypsy woman selling flowers in the rain, the trees reminding me of lives I'd never live.

My grandfather used to say that the happiness we allow ourselves is little more than a dead man's suit. An old soiled hat. It sits next to the glove that doesn't fit anymore, curled around an invisible fist that was last seen pummeling the wind. Soon there is nothing. Stillness among steel and stone. Not even wind, only a string of lost birds plowing the azure. So we sit and wait for the mail that comes on time or it doesn't. Inside, maybe a stone or an overripe peach from a faraway country, the box heavy with a clutter of stamps whose letters resemble all that you ever longed for.

*

My grandfather used to say that a good suit and a good hat should last you a lifetime. But he would often forget his hat and had the inclination to walk out and get stuck in rainstorms without an umbrella. I know now that he went bareheaded on purpose as if each time he'd just fallen in love for the first time and nothing else mattered, or it never did; a dead man wandering in the pouring rain.

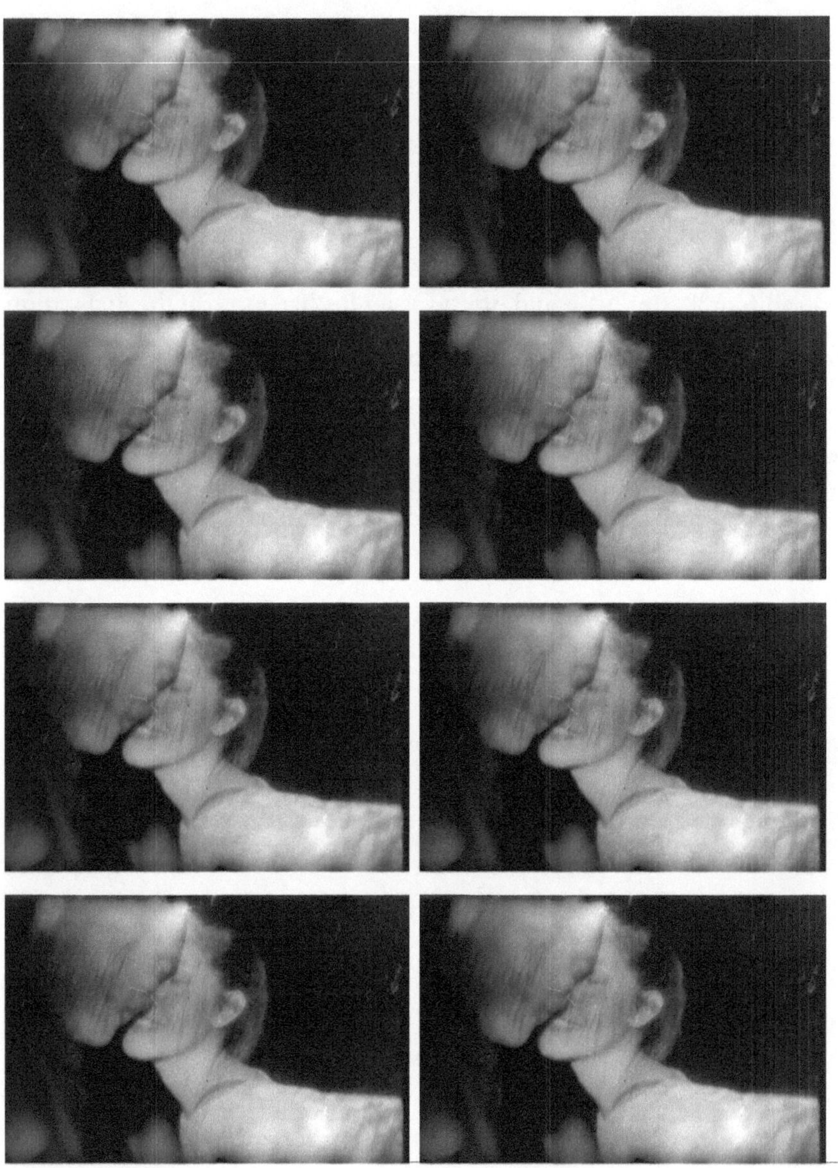

I can still remember endless summer nights out on the steps cracking sunflower seeds and drinking lemon soda. While the rest were on their third can of beer we talked as only children do, with the kind of knowledge one comes to always by chance, from the side and a little bit too late. Our lives were a plotless, yet-to-be-titled Eastern European film where you have to read between the lines because everyone knows that life is beautiful and strange and art is beautiful and strange and most of all a little crooked. All that we cared about existed out there on the cold, spit-stained cement where the moon appeared oil-slick and heavy and the sky belonged to nine-year-olds who thought they knew everything there is to know. How many nights like those do we still have stashed in our back pockets? How many are there left to get us through a lifetime without any stars?

Often, inevitably, I think back against will and reason to the same plot of land that burrows into every childhood dream, that broken painting sitting just above the lake and looking down into the hollow of the valley. Wind should be there, should swirl about the head and throw up dust and chaff and the smells of that small life; the sun at its zenith and the hills around me grazed with gold and green grass, the water on the lake making its silence felt softly.

It is all as it should be—the land uneven, clouds gathering above like wings, morning soft as white marble—in this hour of labor when I try to make an art out of life then lay it down at the feet of a temple of dirt. It is all I have and I am falling short of it.

Inside the house there is a bottle, the wine sour, and nothing else. And I want nothing else tonight, not the door fixed that is whining on its hinges, not the smoke-smudge on the walls, not the crowded mirrors taped over with photographs. How long the memory of a glass of wine? How long the scent and shape of each mouth that spoke once before going silent for good?

When I come home I empty what there is of me on a porcelain tray. In all of my pockets there are traces of time—crumbs, lint, coin, folded message, the warmth I am capable of without even trying.

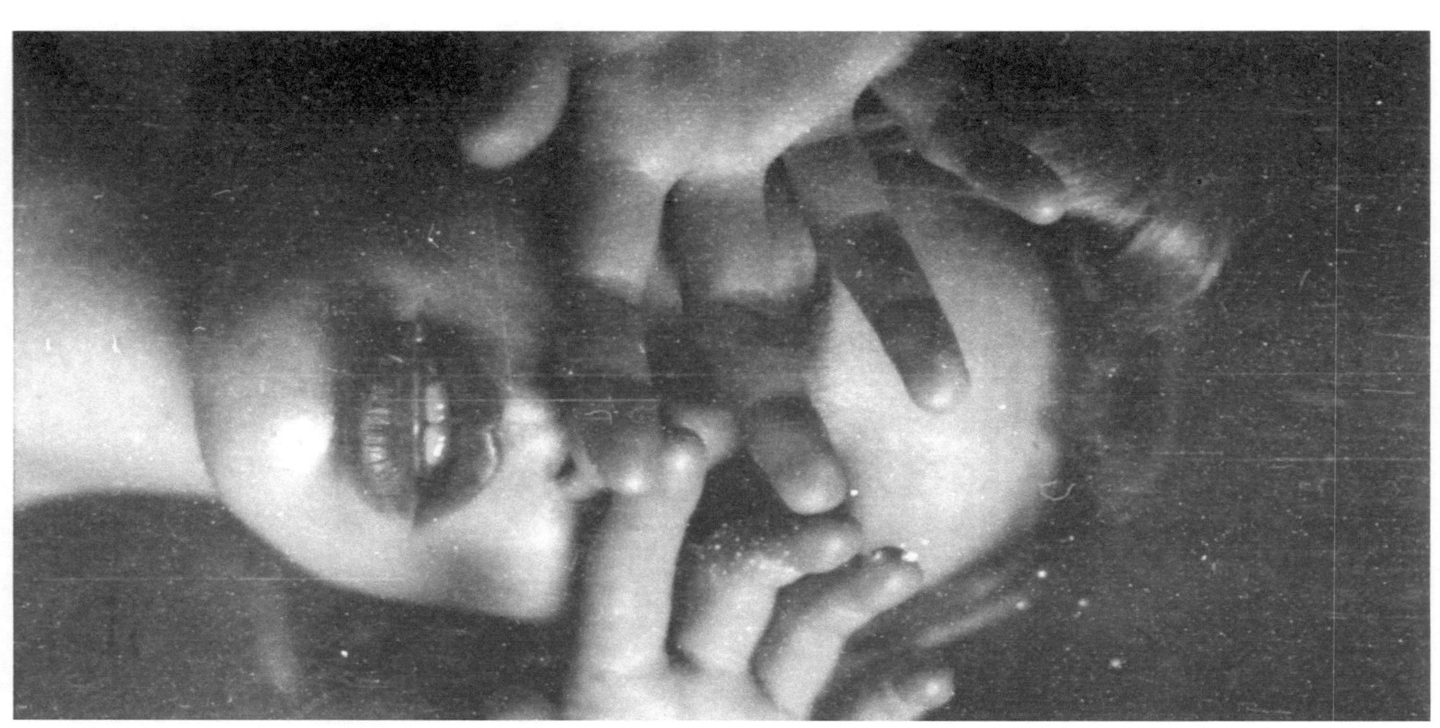

In this obsessive city, a falling apart sort of beautiful, looking down from crumbling balconies at the suicidal morning sprawled as it is along the pavement, bleeding into summer noon. Some appear then disappear to who-knows-what behind the curtains. We layer on masks on top of the masks we've practiced all our lives and with any luck no one will ever spot the difference.

Last night in a dream I opened a wooden box and inside the box was another dream. I cried like a child away from his home for the first time, like a boy who has lost the one and only true love in his life. I walked out on that same balcony and reached for the dark but it drew back like the sea into its infinite shell. Among the constellations lay the words for the morning to come, and they too were weeping.

On nights like these I just want to know that everything will be Ok when the sun comes up. Lie to me if you must. I am done listening to the stars, that bottle we finished just to understand each other as human. It got us nowhere but further away from ourselves. And then once more back again, looking for the lost album of picture-perfect tomorrows.

If I happen to be wrong about all of this then just let it be. We are and always have been willing slaves to the day's circular logic. Let's sleep on that together. Wake up each morning to the turn of the key and throb of engines on the asphalt. The gasoline highway stretching out beyond like a promise. And that too will end, as it must. In a carefree moment when we're busy at the work of happiness. Failing at perfection like ordinary men, like gods.

PART TWO
There is Always Some Harm in Dreaming

A small brass band is playing through the Alley of Roses. Girls are out on the trampled lawn and the boys are playing *futbol*, always *futbol*, their skinny bodies dreaming of something as useless as glory. The girls are getting darker than a farmer's neck, doing nothing, wearing nothing, which drives me crazy, which makes me never want to go home. I want to walk all day and all night dragging myself between dirty buildings in shadow. I don't want to open the door and be in the lamplight all that I am, tired of everything.

It's just after five and the Alley of Roses turns back slowly into gravel and silence, the sun a figment of its former self. A mother wrestles with a boy who does not want to go. I remember when I was like that, how much I used to love being out in the park in the sun running through fields of grass toward nothing in particular.

The girls are rolling up their towels too. One of them slips into a careless dress that rides in increments toward her waist and up over her shoulders where the straps land softly and she's gone. I walk until my feet burn and blister. At home I take off my shoes, draw out the water and bandage the wounds. I sit in the dark, tired of everything.

Nadia, my love, do you remember the years when luxury was that simple white door with a working lock and a mattress on the floor in the corner not even worth stealing? That pair of red enamel mugs with the chipped broken lips blackened from too much scrubbing? Yes, too much scrubbing because you said that you like washing things. I imagine that I will be dead and you will still be washing things, washing by hand even when the joints ache because, as the old saying goes, when a glass breaks at your feet the least you can do is count it as a blessing.

That shouldn't remind me of my mother just now, but it does. In the dark, by candlelight, because the power had gone out, she used to put away plates and cups and fold and refold our one set of linens. What couldn't be folded anymore she tore in thin strips and lay out in bundles in case there was ever a need to tie something together, to stop the bleeding, which she sometimes did.

How long does it take to recognize the cage we are born with? In what acts are we contained? The shy bird's song on summer nights answered in some other dying tree with its immaculate copy. Involuntary and honest, completely out of our hands. The gate is open and the life that beckons is a beautiful one, a charted destiny, while the hour for tea and love has passed so many times we hardly even notice. Sitting there with the empty cup in hand, wishing for a stronger dose of forgetting.

Again the weather is too hot to sleep, too hot to even think about making love. I lie in bed drifting in and out of dreams that tear and split into a thousand dead ends. Dinner on the Champs-Élysées was like that, a summer night loaded with bits of song about our most intimate moments.

Walking back to the hotel I asked, will it always be this way? Sidewalk tables and cigarettes in foreign countries where the accent makes everything appear romantic in the moonlight? You smiled or said nothing and then we made love to occupy the silence.

But maybe it wasn't Paris and it wasn't exactly then. There are gaps like these in every story one can fall through and still be falling. Erase, erase, start over. Always at the beginning. I go to the window and pick up a faint familiar tune. Dream song, for as long as you can tonight, keep on playing that line about a stranger's eyes, her waist in the shape of jazz out in the August sun. That white rose I found and pinned to her hair, though I can't recall how, or when. If it was even summer, as it should have been.

Remember how you used to dance to our favorite album wearing the white skirt that I loved so much? Your eyes would close and you would turn and sway, you would run your hand over the walls, the windowsills, the chair I was sitting on.

Now I'm playing the album all over again just to make that skirt move one last time. Play. Rewind. Replay. Nothing has changed. We've outlived our failures and regrets, the ones we'd nearly forgotten when the final song was done. But that just means we've learned to do without, to spin alone in an empty room.

I turn the record on its back and hear what black lines didn't make the cut. Those B-side chronicles of our simple lives that never saw the light of day. This is the side I'm living now, and it spins and spins, and it's not the same as the other. Tonight, I will leave the lights off and the music on and I will try to read into it, make it more than what it really is.

Play. Rewind. Replay. Four tracks into this brand-new life and nearly halfway to an end everything has changed. The phone booths that I used to call you from each night are gone, the parking meters obsolete, cassette tapes old memory, record players hiss with too much static— all of it a wrinkled soundtrack to our one-bedroom lives and our one-bedroom disappointments, each note reminiscent of the other because we are happiest in symmetries.

Today I walk the streets of Marais, those beautiful and teeming streets, and think about how small everything has become, nothing like the photographs. I take my time getting home. Back at the kitchen table nestled underneath the window I imagine that we can put the record on again and sit there like we used to in the yellow light, dipping into something sweet with a single, tiny spoon.

Maybe that's the secret. Not the light, not the window, not this impossible city. From now on I want to eat everything with a miniature spoon from a miniature plate just to make it last. Then we can play this record until it's all melody and wisdom and the words are winged flights with a heartbeat, familiar like the child-sized streets of the old neighborhoods, like a nook of skin and bone, the perfume of the unadorned body. And if we're up late enough one evening we'll sit and wait in the crooked silence for the hidden track. When it comes, uncertain and untitled, we'll burst into demonic laughter and someone will be laughing back at us, a woman's laughter, looped over and over like a string around your index finger so you won't forget about tomorrow.

What saved us time and again was the way you could stitch together small moments from other people's unhappy seconds. What tricks do you still have in your bottomless bag? Or in the delicate folds of your blouse? As the rest were pinching collars tight around their necks, cursing the night, you would say, "Think of the coming snow, the quiet leading up to." And then somehow you would launch into a story about how warm a hand feels in another's hand, how it would lead you through the park, to the bridge, to the statue, to the now-frozen lake where you would turn and look back and see yourself as a little girl again laughing hysterically when a snowflake tickled your lips.

There's more to it, the story went on after that, undoubtedly to some happy crossroad, but I often stopped listening, feeling sorry for myself. I had dipped my hand into your offering, offering nothing in return but a silence that would not ruin anything. Together we took slow, narcotic breaths that eased the pain of moving on too soon. We always move on too soon. The unknown behind us and in front of us, still saying nothing as if carrying some delicate morsel on the tip of the tongue, savoring the myth. On those nights, in hundreds of windows, the moon cracked open and rearranged itself with each passing cloud.

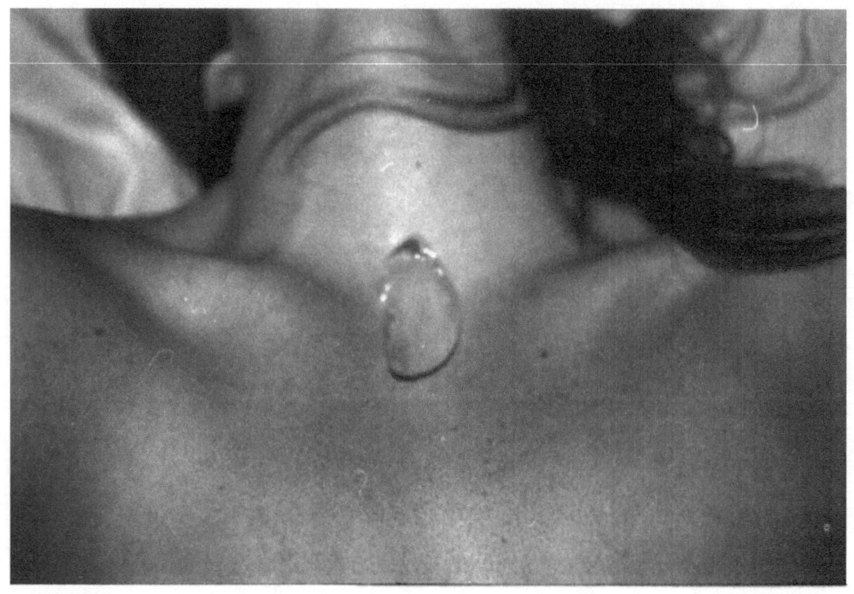

I made a pot of tea tonight and went to the top of the roof just to think of you and how much I don't like to drink tea. Downstairs, two children tall enough to be us at that age were playing in the courtyard wearing toy Napoleon hats and waving at the stars. They will never get any closer. More or less resembling ourselves.

*

The night sugars over like a sacrament with every stolen kiss and every night it isn't ours anymore as it should be. I am lost without you in the sway of leaves. The demented sway of leaves. In all of the reflective storefronts, fragments of architecture, plain, trodden down buildings, miraculous buildings.

*

At this hour, tea in hand, we are all nothing but children, more or less ourselves. Dusk plays on my temples and the air burns with the acrid smell of summer, oil stains and urine in the streets, the blue-green sizzle of the tramline. My face grows numb and falls to my feet like a mask of dead skin and no one even notices—they are all out there forgetting themselves, and who can blame them?

*

Listen to me go on about life. If you care for me, leave whatever you are doing, wherever you are. Pack something light and meet me here halfway across the world. Let the distance shrink tonight, impossible to measure, let it bring us together again. I promise even in the dark we will remain who we appear to be. And let's make love for as long as we can, at least until the end of time returns. If you scream no one will come, I am sure of that. They are in bed watching shadows more or less resembling themselves. And they, too, are waving at the stars.

*

Scream then like you used to when things mattered less because they mean everything now. Scream because we are surrounded by the dead and the deaf. Just once let me not hear the leaves outside turn over in their sleep. Just once, let me forget where I am.

PART THREE
Approximately Us

Sitting on the curb at the bus stop with a book in hand, only the clothes on our backs facing away from the water. And the clouds above the Bosphorus moving with speed in opposite directions, driving all of the seagulls crazy. Like so many days and nights that no one took a picture of because we were in a hurry being somebody else, somewhere else, regardless of the time difference. Like those long weekends of tall drinks under shade of grape vine, roll of die and innuendoes framed against the sunset—lingering hours searching for a single moment to make our own. And always one of us, out of sheer boredom, coming up with different ways to hold a cigarette.

Evenings we walked right through the hour of regret, our effigies nailed to clouds, clothes damp and smelling of the rain. Everything seemed to be swaying to the neon-tinted music, a lazy-honeyed-tempo gesturing the hour. I said, *how small the small things.* I said, *I'm scared when they change and when they stay the same.* On a wall, scratched in black, someone had written, *Learn to look again and see the sky.* And we did— planks of wood nailed to broken windows, wet laundry clothes-pinned to electric wires. A distant radio played something that felt infinite and impossible. All of the shops closed and full of afterhours dreaming. The mannequins down on their hands and knees looking for lost pins and the missing buttons that would put them back together again.

I look outside and see the glass burn with the fever of another heat wave. There are no birds today to fly away and build their nest with everything I've wrapped around my head. I sit Buddha style, occupy the limits of the body, make peace as if these tired bones had been kind to me in another life. It makes me wish for a darkened rain that would coat the windows like armor, like something to hide behind, crawl into, a place to watch the world twist and groan as it ends beautifully by the hour.

Each morning more black tea and sugar cubes to sweeten the morning news. The crowds moving as one between market stalls, doing what the day has asked of them. If you follow them they will lead you through hills of heat and hunger and you will be lost to yourself exactly where you stand. Run instead against the voices and against the hills, to the stone horse that will take you to the palace of honey and flowers. Take care as you pass to avoid the souvenir vendors, the gauntlet of old women marketing their pain. They know more than you think they do.

We expect the shells to tell us more than they know. But the noise of the sea dries out with enough time. And in this desert of sound an old miracle blossoms in geometries of skin. They fit one another like nesting dolls, they intersect below the collarbone, flirt with the blue and shifting hour before sleep. Only the smallest dolls remain unbroken, almost never seen. They can't be pried open—they hide in the folds and stitches, fairy-tale-beautiful; and their painted hearts, the layered life, are woven just above the ribs—they smell of summer and linden trees, the whisper of something simple and sweet.

Barefoot we waded out into the deep until the current took us downstream. On the way we pulled stars from the river and let them fall through our fingers back into the sky. It grew late and the houses on the shore went out one by one, claimed by the silence.

Once you wore a new dress of lotus flowers and portraits of time. When you moved it snagged on a branch and the tear followed us everywhere we went, right down to the places where the first green hour smiles in the face of sleep.

We must have spent hundreds of imaginary miles like that, barely touching, stealing bits and pieces of ourselves when the other wasn't looking. We invented such games because we refused to leave the penumbra of childhood—to step outside old photographs, the doctored emotions, beyond the many delicate and vintage-colored impressions. But the moment turned on us, as every game tends to do, as soon as we had all the rules figured out.

One day, tired of wandering and with the tremor of smoke on your breath, you fixed your eyes on me, dirty with sunlight. You asked, *Are you sure?* I think I said *Yes*, wondering if in the end it really is that simple, if all we need is to be loved.

On a park bench with autumn's wind coming off the river. The flower gardens are gone. The water in the fountains is gone. What pools remain fill quickly to the line with clouds. Birds hunt out of sheer boredom.

You said to me once that songs supposedly about death were really about having loved. And the songs that were supposed to be about love were really about how we are born into sound. What choice then but to undream it all? Pray to speak again the language of ambiguous shapes, to look at two parted lips for the perfect form. For how could we, yet to fully open our eyes, have known anything about limits, that sometimes you could want too much?

Late summer and the cupolas shone across Paris, across Prague, across the waters of Berlin. Below, among candles and bread crumbs we couldn't differentiate between shadows. Each day grew shorter but the clouds lingered on, joined and fell apart, and every animal that floated by looked a little more like us.

Nearly on the other side of autumn now and the radio crawls to a symphonic lisp, nudges time to the edge of a precipice, a familiar absence. With the screen door open I can feel the north air as it winds around the room. I'm at peace with the coming winter, snow that erases doubt.

In another life I imagine we're together again at our favorite restaurant where the stage is vacant save for the plywood musicians being moved into place. An old couple weaves through the soundtrack of another time, another place, somewhere on the fringes of a nation of dreams, by the distant shore, inside the summer of the young.

It's a Sunday afternoon, a lazy matinee, time when it's easy to believe that a star has been born just for you. Some bright cosmic promise out of reach with your name on it. And when it dies, as all promises do in the end, there is still a wish to be made. A not-yet-bitter maybe.

The plywood orchestra is ready to take its place. The maestro is done winding his watch. He sets it for another time and another place, somewhere in the wrinkle of a vintage-rose horizon, by the naked shore inside the summer of the lost. Lost—as everyone who comes here. As anyone who's ever listened to the blues and knows the loneliness of holding hands under a table as the band begins to play.

Then Sunday evening, walking home, small flourishes of blue and those who've figured out a way to dance to the sound of it. To grab it by the arm and swing it around once in a while. No song, no stage, the moon winding down as they linger a bit longer, their one and only thought tethered to the stars; those impossibly distant lights, each one beautiful and strange, just as we used to be.

Teknari is a Binghamton, NY-based artist whose recent photographic and digital works explore the potential of chance and random occurrence to add nuance and depth to personal expression through the use of his own handmade silver gelatin emulsion film. He believes that despite the full presence of the artist in the process, photography is a subconscious effort on the part of both photographer and model, becoming ultimately an act of liberation from the confines of convention.

Fomite

More Odd Birds from Fomite...
Micheal Breiner — *the way none of this happened*
Bill Davis — *Cheap Gestures*
J. C. Ellefson — *Under the Influence: Shouting Out to Walt*
David Ross Gunn — *Cautionary Chronicles*
Andrei Guriuanu & Teknari — *The Darkest City*
Gail Holst-Warhaft — *The Fall of Athens*
Daniil Kharms — *Connections* (translator Roger Lebovitz, artitst Delia Robinson)
Roger Lebovitz — *A Guide to the Western Slopes and the Outlying Area*
Roger Lebovitz — *Twenty-two Instructions for Near Survival*
dug Nap— *Artsy Fartsy*
dug Nap— *Friends*
Delia Bell Robinson — *A Shirtwaist Story*
Claire Russell — *Dear Mr. Thoreau*
Peter Schumann — *A Child's Deprimer*
Peter Schumann — *All*
Peter Schumann — *All, Nothing, Nothing at All*
Peter Schumann — *Bedsheet Mitigations*
Peter Schumann — *Belligerent & Not So Belligerent Slogans from the
Possibilitarian Arsenal*
Peter Schumann — *Bread & Sentences*
Peter Schumann — *Charlotte Salomon*
Peter Schumann — *Declaration of Light*
Peter Schumann — *Diagonal Man Theory + Praxis, Volumes One and Two*
Peter Schumann — *Faust 3*
Peter Schumann — *Handouts and Obligations*
Peter Schumann — *Planet Kasper, Volumes One and Two*
Peter Schumann — *We*

Writing a review on social media sites for readers will help the progress of independent publishing. To submit a review, go to the book page on any of the sites and follow the links for reviews. Books from independent presses rely on reader-to-reader communications.

For more information or to order any of our books, visit:
http://www.fomitepress.com/our-books.html